# Vinnie the Dove

Vinnie loves to dive in water, but it always makes him so cold! Join him on his mission get warmed up.

This picture book targets the /v/ sound and is part of *Speech Bubbles 2*, a series of picture books that target specific speech sounds within the story.

The series can be used for children receiving speech therapy, for children who have a speech sound delay/disorder, or simply as an activity for children's speech sound development and/or phonological awareness. They are ideal for use by parents, teachers or caregivers.

Bright pictures and a fun story create an engaging activity perfect for sound awareness.

Picture books are sold individually, or in a pack. There are currently two packs available – *Speech Bubbles 1* and *Speech Bubbles 2.* Please see further titles in the series for stories targeting other speech sounds.

**Melissa Palmer** is a Speech Language Therapist. She worked for the Ministry of Education, Special Education in New Zealand from 2008 to 2013, with children aged primarily between 2 and 8 years of age. She also completed a diploma in children's writing in 2009, studying under author Janice Marriott, through the New Zealand Business Institute. Melissa has a passion for articulation and phonology, as well as writing and art, and has combined these two loves to create *Speech Bubbles*.

# What's in the pack?

User Guide

Vinnie the Dove

Rick's Carrot

Harry the Hopper

Have You Ever Met a Yeti?

Zack the Buzzy Bee

Asher the Thresher Shark

Catch That Chicken!

Will the Wolf

Magic Licking Lollipops

Jasper the Badger

Platypus and Fly

The Dragon Drawing War

# Vinnie the Dove

## Targeting the /v/ Sound

Melissa Palmer

Routledge
Taylor & Francis Group

LONDON AND NEW YORK

First published 2021
by Routledge
2 Park Square, Milton Park, Abingdon, Oxon OX14 4RN

and by Routledge
52 Vanderbilt Avenue, New York, NY 10017

*Routledge is an imprint of the Taylor & Francis Group, an informa business*

© 2021 Melissa Palmer

*British Library Cataloguing-in-Publication Data*
A catalogue record for this book is available from the British Library

*Library of Congress Cataloging-in-Publication Data*
A catalog record has been requested for this book

ISBN: 978-1-138-59784-6 (set)
ISBN: 978-0-367-64849-7 (pbk)
ISBN: 978-1-003-12655-3 (ebk)

Typeset in Calibri
by Newgen Publishing UK

Printed in the UK by Severn, Gloucester on responsibly sourced paper

# Vinnie the Dove

Vinnie the do**v**e loved to go di**v**ing in the ri**v**er. The problem was **V**innie would get **v**ery cold.

One day after di**v**ing in the ri**v**er, **V**innie started to shi**v**er
**v-v-v-v-v-v-v-v-v-v-v**.

He needed to get warm, so he do**v**e into a ca**v**e. But someone else lived in the ca**v**e …

Da**v**e the bea**v**er. He was a **v**ery mean and **v**icious bea**v**er. He threw fi**v**e rocks at **V**innie. So **V**innie flew away, shi**v**ering **v-v-v-v-v-v-v-v-v-v-v**.

**V**innie found a house. Inside the house was an o**v**en, and he crawled inside.

The o**v**en was **v**ery hot and hurt **V**innie's feathers. He flew away shi**v**ering **v-v-v-v-v-v-v-v-v-v-v**.

Vinnie found a glove, and covered his wings with it. He felt so much warmer!

**V**innie tried to fly away, but couldn't get **v**ery far with his wings co**v**ered, so he took the glo**v**e off.

**V**innie found a **v**est and put it on. Now **V**innie was **v**ery warm, with his body co**v**ered and his wings free to fly.

"I'm so **v**ery cle**v**er!" **V**innie said, and flew back to the ri**v**er.